Lily and the
Polar Bears

Jion Sheibani

ff

FABER & FABER

One day, Lily was playing on the beach with her grandpa when she spotted **something in the distance . . .**

POLAR
BEARS!

Lots of **polar bears!**
All **floating** on pieces of **melting ice.**

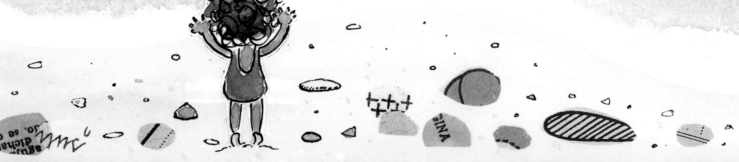

"Hullo!" they said as they clambered onto the shore. "We're very sorry to bother you but **our homes have melted** and we've nowhere to stay. Can you help us?"

Lily thought for a moment. "Well, we do have a
special room for guests – and a tree house!
Come with us!"

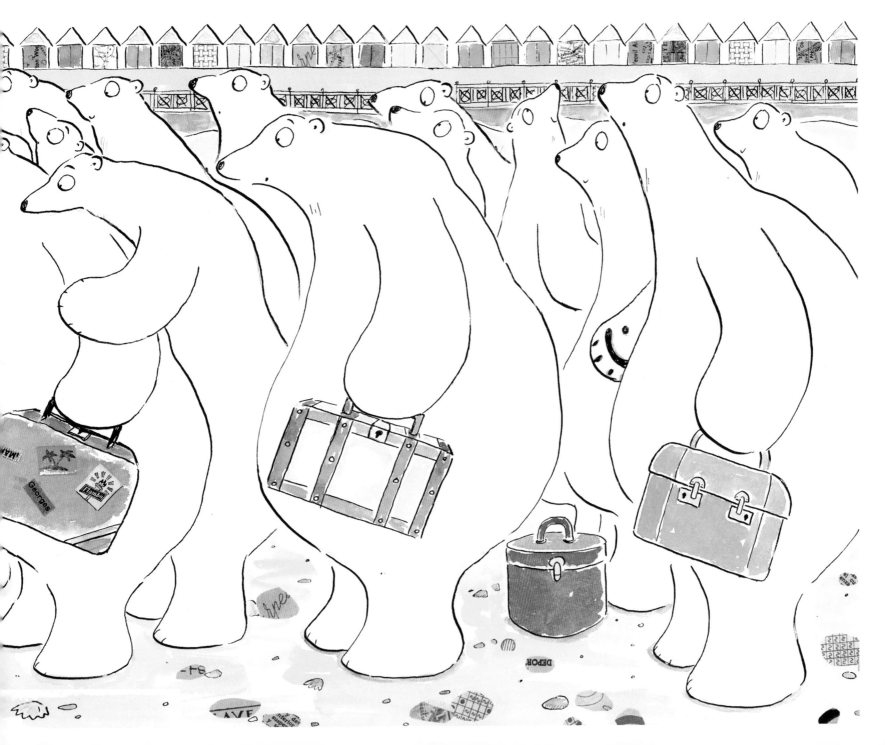

The polar bears followed Lily and her grandpa back to Lily's house.

When she opened the door, Lily's mum nearly fainted.
"Goodness me!" she said. "Where did you lot come from?!"
Then she invited the polar bears in for tea and cake.

The polar bears told Lily's mum all about their long and dangerous **journey from the Arctic.**

Afterwards, they all sat down to dinner.

Thankfully, Lily's mum always had plenty of **fish fingers**, **chips** and **ice cream** in the freezer – just in case they had guests!

When the polar bears had **tidied the table** and helped to wash the dishes, it was time to get **ready for bed**.

Then they **huddled together** in Lily's den so that she could read them a **bedtime story.**

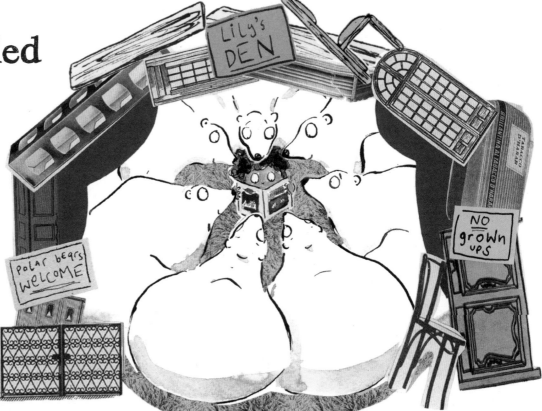

Eventually, when they had found enough space for everyone to sleep, they said **goodnight**.

The polar bears went **out like a light.**

The next day, Lily took the polar bears out **into the town.**

The children were *very* excited.

The **grown-ups** really *weren't*.

They thought the polar bears
took up **too much room** . . .

or that they might **eat** them!

But in time,
people realised
that the polar bears
were **kind**.

and **FUN!**

Soon, the polar bears got their own **flats** and **jobs**.

There were polar
bear **builders,**

polar bear **teachers**

and polar bear
postmen.

There were also polar bear **policemen**,

polar bear **footballers**,

polar bear **dancers**

and **singers**.

Some polar bears opened their own shops.

Some polar bears even became
ASTRONAUTS!

And the most **wonderful thing** of all was *everyone* felt at home.

For Philippe

FABER & FABER has published children's books since 1929. Some of our very first publications included *Old Possum's Book of Practical Cats* by T. S. Eliot starring the now world-famous Macavity, and *The Iron Man* by Ted Hughes. Our catalogue at the time said that 'it is by reading such books that children learn the difference between the shoddy and the genuine'. We still believe in the power of reading to transform children's lives.

First published in the UK in 2018
by Faber and Faber Limited
Bloomsbury House, 74–77 Great Russell Street,
London WC1B 3DA

Text and illustration © Jion Sheibani, 2018

ISBN 978–0–571–33776–7

Printed in China

The moral rights of Jion Sheibani have been asserted.

A CIP record for this book is available from the British Library

10 9 8 7 6 5 4 3 2 1